"Witty, wise and occasionally wicked, nobody tells a story like the great Tony McGowan" PHIL EARLE

"It is becoming difficult to find fresh superlatives to describe Anthony McGowan's writing, but *The Beck* is an absolutely pitch-perfect delight ... There is an authentic gritty reality underlying the humour, but ultimately this is a celebration of both intergenerational familial love and of the nature in our own backyard. Simply wonderful!" JOY COURT, LOVEREADING4KIDS

"There is not a word out of place in this perfectly crafted, wise and extremely witty novella about caring for the natural world" *THE BOOKSELLER*

"A timeless, exquisitely crafted tale of resistance and standing up for what's right" WATERSTONES

"Anthony McGowan strikes again! Hugely sensitive, very amusing yet accessible in the way of all quality Barrington Stoke" TERESA CREMIN

"*The Beck* is constantly entertaining, equally thought-provoking, and proof yet again of Anthony McGowan's wonderful storytelling skills. Full of hope and humour, there's heart and soul on every page" KEITH GRAY

"Anthony McGowan is a miraculous storyteller. He has the power to move you, make you laugh out loud, cringe in embarrassment and recoil in disgust in a single page. This book is a small piece of magic from the mind of a very great writer" KATYA BALEN

"An utterly brilliant, funny and inspiring novel ... showcases McGowan's talent as a wordsmith" *THE* ~~BOOKSELLER~~

THE
BECK

ANTHONY McGOWAN

Barrington Stoke

Published by Barrington Stoke
An imprint of HarperCollins*Publishers*
1 Robroyston Gate, Glasgow, G33 1JN

www.barringtonstoke.co.uk

HarperCollins*Publishers*
Macken House, 39/40 Mayor Street Upper,
Dublin 1, DO1 C9W8, Ireland

First published in 2025

ISBN 978-0-00-872229-6

10 9 8 7 6 5 4 3 2

Printed and Bound in the UK using 100% Renewable Electricity
at Martins the Printers Ltd

This book contains FSC™ certified paper and other controlled
sources to ensure responsible forest management.

For more information visit: www.harpercollins.co.uk/green

Contents

1 Dumped   1

2 A Rude Word   6

3 How to Wear a Cat   15

4 The Adventure Begins – Slowly   19

5 The Beck   21

6 A Death in the Family   28

7 The Burial of the Dead   31

8 Toothache   38

9 The Killer Worm   42

10 No Trespassing!   48

11 The Cunning Plan   51

12 Bumface and Dried Bogey   56

13 Home Life   61

14 Plan 2   64

15	On the Bus	68
16	Terrible Discovery	76
17	Last Words	85
18	Hospital	87
19	Decisions	89
20	Prep	93
21	Phase 1	97
22	Level 1 Boss	100
23	Hopes are Crushed	105
24	Phase 2	112
25	Phase 3	116
26	Catastrophe, Triumph, Disaster	120
27	The Bogey Man	123
28	The Darkest Hour	128
29	Back to the Hospital	133
30	The End	139

*To the Wyke Beck, and the people,
young and old, who live on its banks as
it winds its way through East Leeds*

One

Dumped

"Oh, look," said Mum, trying to make her voice sound bright and happy. "There's a baby sheep!"

"Lamb," I said in a flat voice.

"What?" Mum asked.

"A baby sheep is a lamb."

"I know that," Mum replied. "But saying 'lamb' makes it sound like, well, dinner. And it's just there. In the field. Playing."

I was sitting in the back of our car with my head pressed against the window, watching the boring fields go by. I liked feeling the bumps and vibrations on my forehead. They helped take my mind off what was coming up. And what was coming up was being dumped at Grandad's house.

"I don't want to go to Grandad's," I said. My voice sounded whiny and annoying even to me.

"It'll be fine," said Dad. "Anyway, it's only for a couple of hours while me and your mum sort some things out in town."

"But there's nothing to do," I complained. "And Grandad's house smells funny."

"And there's his wig," added my mum. I could tell she was trying not to laugh.

Grandad's wig was famous. Not "on the news" famous, but famous in our family.

"Don't," said my dad. "He's not been the same since Granny … went. Your grandad's let himself go a bit. Granny kept him more … normal."

"Great," I said. "And you're dumping me there for the whole day."

"Two hours," Dad corrected me, "then we'll be done, and we'll pick you up."

The closer we got to Grandad's, the more I dreaded it. I only ever got left with Grandad when all the other babysitting options were used up. It was like when you look in the cupboard for some

biscuits, hoping for maybe a Jaffa Cake or a Jammy Dodger, and all you find is a cracker. Or nothing.

The countryside turned into the town. All too soon we were in Grandad's estate, with its windy streets and rain in the air. Houses made of red brick that had a sickly wet look even when it hadn't been raining, as if the houses were sweating out some kind of poison. Half of the gardens had old junk dumped in them. Fridges, mattresses, a microwave, a doll without a head. A head without a doll.

"It's worse than ever," said Mum.

"I remember when it was all right," said Dad. "I loved growing up round here. All the stuff we got up to ..."

Dad was always going on about the things he used to do when he was a kid. Like building dens, bonfires, fireworks. All the things he doesn't let me do.

There was no drive or garage at Grandad's, so we parked in the street, in between a white van and the skeleton of another car without any doors or wheels. The white van was filthy, and someone

had written "cLeAn mE" on the back of it in the muck. Someone else had written some bad words underneath that as an answer – most likely the bloke who owned the van. You can probably guess what it said.

"Come on then," said Dad, and we got out of the car.

"I'll stay sat here," said Mum.

"Suit yourself," said Dad.

There was a little bit of garden running up to the front door. It was neat compared to some of the other front gardens. There were some flowers and a bird table with a string bag of peanuts hanging from it.

Dad pressed the bell, but there was no *ding-dong*, so then he knocked at the door.

Still nothing.

Dad tutted and knocked harder. Suddenly, there was some frantic barking.

"Has Grandad got a dog?" I asked hopefully.

"Dunno," said Dad, looking puzzled. "It's the first I've heard about it if he has."

He knocked again. After more barking, finally a muffled voice came from inside.

"I'm on the bog!"

Dad looked at me, and I looked at Dad.

"We're going to be late," Mum yelled from the car. Dad checked his watch, then knocked again.

"Just leave it on the doorstep," came the voice.

"It's us, not a bloody delivery!" shouted Dad at the door.

Then Mum honked the car horn.

BEEEEEEEEEEEP

"I've gotta go," Dad said. "We can't miss this appointment. It's important."

He rushed to the car and honked goodbye on the horn as he was driving off.

BEEP.

Two

A Rude Word

The barking had stopped, but I could still hear
a heavy creature moving behind the door. It
sounded a bit strange. You expect dogs to scurry
and scamper, but this was more plodding than
scampering.

I glanced around the street while I was waiting.
A woman pushed a pram along the pavement. She
looked skinny and fierce, with her hair pulled up
into a ponytail that exploded out of the top of her
head. But when she saw me, she smiled, and her
face turned soft and pretty. As she went past me,
I saw that the pushchair didn't have a baby in it
but cans and bottles.

A minute later, I heard the toilet flush. I knocked
at the door, which set the dog off barking again.

"Shut the heck up, Rude Word!" said Grandad.

Rude Word? I thought. That couldn't be right. That wasn't a name. Maybe he'd said "Rudolph", like the reindeer. But that was a terrible name for a dog. Unless he had a red nose?

I was thinking about this when the door opened and Grandad was there. He had a shirt and tie on, and a sort of a suit that appeared to be made out of old carpet. He didn't have his famous wig on, so I could see his baldy head, with a few greasy grey strands of hair stretched across it.

The dog was standing behind him. I say "dog", but it was like no dog I'd ever seen. He had a massive head that looked like it came off some other animal – a hyena or baboon or something. His body was round, and his legs were short. Not short like a sausage dog but more like a bulldog. And he only had three of them. The leg at the front on the left side wasn't there. He had half a tail, which he was wagging, or trying to wag. His fur was mainly black, with some random tufts of ginger.

Rudolph was the ugliest dog I'd ever seen.

Grandad stared down at me with his pale, watery eyes like he was trying to work out who I was.

Then he said, "Oh, ay up, Kyle. What you doing here?"

"Dad dropped me," I replied. "He said he'd arranged it with you."

"Did he? Maybe he did. He's always arranging something, your dad."

The dog was ugly, but he looked pretty friendly. He came over, and I put my hand down, and he sniffed it.

"Is that your dog?" I said.

"What? Yeah. Who else's would it be?" Grandad said. "Do you think I nicked him? Who'd steal a dog like that? Anyway, come in and get comfy."

The hallway floor was littered with leaflets and unopened letters. The ones that are brown with a window for the name and address. Grandad kicked them out of the way, and I followed him.

Inside, the house smelled a bit like school dinners and a bit like wet dog.

"Sit thee down in there," said Grandad, "and I'll put kettle on and find thee summat to eat."

"I'm not really hungry," I said, worried what Grandad might find.

"Course you are. Young lads are always hungry."

I sat on the sofa in the living room. There were piles of old newspapers on the floor. The walls were covered in that stuff that looks like swirls of mashed potato. The carpet was yellow and brown, like it had been puked on by someone who only ate bananas and gravy. There was a telly in the corner from the olden days – square not flat and with buttons instead of a remote. There was an old armchair in the corner with some cushions that looked like a pile of dead bodies. A black cat was asleep on it. Or maybe it was dead too.

I'd only been there a minute, but I thought I was going to literally die of boredom and join the cat. But then Grandad's dog came and sat in front of me, staring at my face as if he was hoping I'd give him something.

I'd been excited about the idea of a dog. But the real thing right in front of me wasn't that great. The dog's missing leg and half a tail freaked me out a bit, not to mention the fact he was so ugly. I couldn't imagine him doing any tricks. Or maybe just not falling over counted as a trick as he only had three legs?

I patted his head. I thought it made a hollow sound, like an empty shoebox, but it might have been my imagination.

I remembered coming here when Granny was still alive. It had been good then, especially when my aunts and uncles and cousins were there. The place was always full of noise. People arguing, making up, laughing, arguing again. But I'd been a bit afraid of Uncle Jimmy, because he was pretty rough in a friendly way. He used to pick me up and swing me round like I was a doll.

My dad seemed a bit embarrassed about him. Uncle Jimmy drives a lorry, but Dad's a Maths teacher. My mum works in HR, which stands for "Human Resources", but I've got no idea what that means.

Grandad came in with two cups of tea. I
don't even like tea, but I didn't say anything. He
handed me one, then put his cup down on the floor
and went back to the kitchen. While he was out,
Rudolph went and sniffed at his cup. He took a
couple of licks at it. Then Grandad came back with
a plate. On the plate, there was half a sausage roll.
But at least it had been cut in half and not just
eaten halfway.

"Get that down you," Grandad said to me. "You
look like you need building up. I expect your mam
and dad feed you on lentils and beansprouts."

"Grandad?" I said.

"Yeah?"

"Why's Rudolph only got three legs?"

"Who?"

"Rudolph ..." I pointed at the dog.

"He's not called Rudolph," Grandad said.

"Oh, sorry. I thought that's what you called
him ... So what's his name?"

Grandad looked a bit embarrassed.

"Well, he's called Rude Word," he said.

And I'd thought Rudolph was a weird name.

"OK, then why has Rude Word only got three legs?" I asked.

"He was sitting in a corner chewing a bone, and when he got up, he only had three legs."

"That's not funny, Grandad."

"Please yourself. I don't know why he's got three legs," Grandad said. "He was like that when I found him. And I didn't ask him about it in case he was sensitive on the subject and didn't want to talk about it."

"Oh, right. Er, Grandad?"

"Yeah?"

"Why's he called Rude Word?" I asked.

"Well, I'll have to explain how I came by him. You see, I opened the door one day, and there he was, sitting there. I was that shocked that I said, er, a rude word."

"Which one?"

"Never you mind. I don't want your mam saying I've been teaching you bad words. Anyway, when I said this rude word, the dog looked up at me like I'd said his name. That made me think that it really was his name."

Grandad paused for a moment and picked up his cup of tea.

"I looked up and down the street to see if someone was searching for him," he went on. "But there was no one there. I left him, thinking he'd wander off to where he came from. And when I came back from the shops, he was still there. Hadn't moved a muscle. So I opened the door and said, 'Come in then,' and he did, and he's never left. Once he'd settled in, I realised I couldn't call him by his original name. I couldn't shout it out in the park, that bad word, could I? People wouldn't like it. So I thought I'd just call him 'Rude Word', and he soon got used to it."

"And no one ever came for him?" I said.

"Nah. I put a flyer on a few lampposts, but no one seemed to want a dog with three legs. He didn't look healthy when he showed up. Not just his leg. All of him. He was just bone held together with hair."

"What kind of dog is he anyway?"

"All sorts," Grandad replied. "Probably a bit of everything you could think of. Apart from poodle, thank god."

He took a sip of his tea and pulled a face. Then he said a rude word and went off to make another cup. While he was out, I gave Rude Word the half a sausage roll.

Three

How to Wear a Cat

"How long did your dad say he was leaving you here for?" asked Grandad when he came back.

"Two hours," I replied.

"You sound dead happy about it."

"Sorry."

"Nah, I get it," Grandad said. "What young feller wants to spend two hours with an old codger like me?"

I didn't say anything.

"But that doesn't mean we can't have a bit of fun."

"Your telly's a hundred years old and there's no internet," I said.

Grandad sighed.

"You don't need the telly or the internet to have a laugh."

"I suppose you're going to tell me that they didn't have telly when you were my age."

"I'm seventy-six, not a hundred and seventy-six, you cheeky get! Anyways, what you need is an adventure."

That woke me up a bit.

"Where? How?" I asked.

"You don't have to go to the Arctic or the Amazon to be an explorer. You can be one right here, in Leeds!"

"Yeah, right. How can we have an adventure round here?"

"Well, you follow me, and you'll soon learn!" Grandad said. "Just hang on a sec."

I'd forgotten about the cat asleep on the armchair. But now Grandad bent down, picked it up and put it on his baldy head.

It wasn't a cat.

It was the famous wig.

Grandad used to work as an Elvis impersonator at the weekend, so maybe it was once an Elvis wig –

you know, with a shape to it – but now it looked like a dead cat on top of his shiny head. It was all I could do not to burst out laughing.

"Grandad, are you really going out with that … um …?"

"What you on about?" he said.

I pointed at the wig.

Grandad looked behind him as if I'd been pointing at the wall.

"Nowt there, you daft lad. You must be seeing things. Now, come on. There's worlds to discover."

While we were speaking, Rude Word looked at us like he was trying to work out what we were saying. Now Grandad said the first word he really could understand.

"Walkies!"

The dog staggered up onto his three paws, his stubby tail wagging so fast it was a blur.

Grandad led the way into the kitchen and out of the back door, picking up a knobbly walking stick on the way.

"Have you got a bad leg, Grandad?" I asked.

"Nah. Not really. I just like to use it to point at stuff. Like if someone asks you the way to somewhere. And I can shake it in a rage, when the mood takes me. Life's better with a stick."

Four

The Adventure Begins – Slowly

Now we were in Grandad's back garden. There was a hedge around it, and some grass, and it sloped down to a low wall. Grandad stepped over the wall, with me behind him. Rude Word followed us, slowly.

"Should I help him?" I asked Grandad.

"Nay, lad. He'll get there. If you can do a thing on your own, it's best to. When you can't, then reach out for a helping hand. But if you can manage, manage."

I watched as Rude Word got himself over the wall without too much trouble.

Beyond the wall, there was a lumpy field of grass. Not exactly the sort of place where you could have much of an adventure.

We had to go slow because of Rude Word.
Apart from him hobbling on three legs, he did a lot
of snuffling around, and he kept stopping to have
a wee.

I was starting to think that as far as exciting
expeditions went, this was quite low on the list –
just a bit higher than going to the dentist.

"Where we off to, Grandad?" I asked as we
trudged on.

"See down there?" He pointed with his stick the
way we were going. At the end of the field, there
was a line of scruffy little trees and bushes.

"Yeah."

"Beyond the trees, there's what we're after."

Five

The Beck

We carried on, and after a while I heard a trickle of water. You can't hear running water without feeling a bit of excitement.

"What is it?" I asked.

"That's the beck," Grandad replied.

"What's a beck?"

"*What's a beck?* Does tha know nowt, lad?"

"I know loads of stuff, but I don't know that."

Grandad sighed.

"A beck's a stream," he said.

"You should have said that then."

"A stream somewhere else is a stream," Grandad went on. "A stream here is a beck."

"Whatever."

Grandad tutted. "Come on – let's have a gander."

"A what?"

"A gander. It means a look, you daft lad."

We pushed past some bushes, and there it was – the stream. Or beck. The water was brown with white froth. Nothing special. There were a few bits of waterweed waving in it like green hair. I might just have been able to jump across it with a decent run-up.

"Let's see what's what," said Grandad. "Get yer shoes and socks off."

"What? Really? Mum will kill me."

"No, she won't."

Then Grandad kicked off his battered old shoes. His big toe stuck out of a hole in his sock.

"Come here, Kyle," he said.

I was a bit worried that he was going to ask me to peel his manky socks off for him. I think I'd have puked at that. But all he wanted was to put his hand on me for balance while he did it.

Grandad managed to get his socks off without falling in, which was a miracle. Then he rolled his

trousers up and stepped into the beck. The water came halfway up to his bony knees.

Rude Word was watching all this like a person would watch the telly.

"Come on then, lad," Grandad said.

The water didn't look too clean. I knew I'd get dirt on my trousers and Mum would have a go at me. But I didn't want Grandad to think I was scared. So I kicked off my trainers and pulled my socks off and slowly put my foot in the water.

It was cold, but not so cold it gave me a shock. The bottom was slimy with waterweeds, and I could feel the mud underneath, as well as small stones. It was just a weedy little stream, so I was surprised to feel the current in it pushing against the backs of my legs.

"Feels good, dunt it?" said Grandad, grinning, his false teeth glinting in the sun.

"Not bad."

I put my other foot down very carefully. The current made me wobble, and Grandad offered his hand, but I didn't need to take it.

"Good lad," he said. "Right, let's see what we can find."

He stooped and peered into the water.

"Might be a stickleback or two. And a bullhead," Grandad muttered. "This is their kind of lodgings. Maybe an eel."

"Why have you never taken me here before, Grandad?"

"I never thought to. For years, the beck's been more of a sewer than a river, ever since your dad were a lad. All kinds of crap in there, and the only living things were the rats. But they've cleaned it up now. The beck's breathing again. Life's back."

"Who fixed it?" I asked.

"Council made a bit of an effort. Some local people. Got a few quid from various charities and do-gooders, for once doing some good. I'm not saying David Attenborough's going to make one of his programmes about it, but there's life again in the old girl."

Grandad never took his eyes off the water as he spoke, and then suddenly his whole body

seemed to get a jolt of electric energy, and he shoved his big hands in.

"What is it?" I asked.

"Bullhead!"

Grandad drew his hands out of the beck and held them dripping under my face. Then he opened them slowly, making a big deal out of it, like he was performing a magic trick. I thought he was just fooling with me and that there'd be nothing inside, but I was wrong. It was a fish as long as his thumb. The fish was mottled and blotchy, coloured different kinds of brown, and it had a big fat face and bulging lips. It looked a bit silly but also awesome and really old, like it'd been in the beck so long it'd remember dinosaurs coming down to drink.

Then Grandad closed his hand around the bullhead, put it to his mouth and swallowed.

"No!" I yelled.

Grandad chuckled, opened his hand and showed me the fish, then he put it back in the beck.

"Got you!" he said.

I was smiling and annoyed at the same time, and I went a bit red because he'd tricked me so easily. But I didn't really mind. The beck was OK.

Then Grandad began to turn the stones over gently with his rough hands. After the third stone, he said, "Yes!" Like before, he put his hands under the water, and this time he came out with a little black monster.

"Is that a scorpion?" I asked, cos it looked just like that, its claws snapping. It had a curved tail divided into segments, just like a scorpion, but I couldn't see its sting. It had long antennae waving out of its head.

"Nay, lad! He's a crayfish. They're dead rare now. They only live where the water's clean."

"Can I hold him?" I asked.

"Aye. Just watch them pincers. Bite your finger off, easy."

"Really?"

"No!" Grandad said. "Give you a little nip, that's all. It'd smart a tad, but you could still count up to ten afterwards, no bother. Hold your hand flat."

I put my hand out, and the crayfish crawled onto it. He was as long as my little finger. Heavier than I thought he would be. The crayfish moved his claws around, trying to find something to pinch.

"Mind, he's feisty," Grandad added.

His spiky feet made my skin tingle.

"Best put the little chap back now. Shouldn't really have taken him out, but I wanted to show you the wonder of him. These fellers have been snapping them claws a hundred million years an' more. Think of that."

I stooped and dipped my hand under the flowing beck water, and the crayfish slipped into the murk.

Six

A Death in the Family

"Well, lad," said Grandad, looking properly happy for the first time as we stood in the beck. It was the deep kind of happy that didn't show with a smile or a laugh but that you could feel like the warmth coming off a fire. "I can see your feet are turning blue. Let's go have a cuppa."

Grandad turned round in the beck, but for the first time he looked unsteady as the current caught him. He tottered and staggered forward. I thought he was going to fall face-first into the water, but Grandad just managed to stay on his feet. But as his head jerked forward, the old wig fell off, splashed into the water and went floating off down the stream.

"Bloody hell," he said. "Grab it!"

I lunged for the wig.

I missed.

The current had it, and the wig gathered speed, almost like it was alive and wanted to escape.

Rude Word had been lying there happily all the time but now realised that something was happening. He started barking and turning in circles on his back legs.

"Move yoursen!" screamed Grandad, along with some bad words. "Use this," he said to me, chucking his stick.

I caught the stick and then scampered up and along the muddy bank, chasing the wig in my bare feet. I managed to get ahead of my hairy prey, then lunged and speared it with the stick. I felt good, like I'd caught some dangerous wild animal, and I gave a yell of victory.

But I also felt a bit sad. As if the wig truly were a wild creature and should be allowed to roam free.

I brought it back to Grandad on the end of the stick, dripping and covered in weed.

I thought for a moment that Grandad was going to start crying.

"Look at state of you, poor old lad," he said to the wig.

Then he took it and shook off the weeds and muck. He wrung it out like a dishcloth and put it back on his head.

"Right," he said, cheerful once more, "let's go and put that kettle on."

*

Later, when Dad came to collect me, Grandad said to me, "Let's do this again. Explore a bit further next time. See what we can find."

"Yeah," I said. "That'd be great."

"Was it all right at your grandad's?" Dad asked in the car on the way home.

"It was OK," I said. "Grandad's got a dog with three legs."

But there wasn't much chat in the car. Mum was quiet. Then I caught sight of her face reflected in the driver's mirror.

Her eyes were red.

Seven

The Burial of the Dead

It was two weeks later when I next went back to Grandad's. Mum and Dad had another of their appointments in town.

For some reason, the beck had got into my head the way that sometimes a tune gets into your head and won't let go. It was like an earworm thing, only this was a mindworm – the idea of the beck winding across the dirty old town. A secret that just a few people knew about, yet there for anyone to see.

Grandad opened the door wearing one of those hats that French people wear. A beret. He had a serious look on his face, sort of blank and drained of emotion.

"Kyle lad," Grandad said. "Just in time."

"What for?"

I was hoping for another adventure.

"Funeral."

"What? Whose …?" I asked.

"Just follow me."

I went in and then straight out into the back garden. There was a hole dug on the edge of the lawn.

It was then that I began to feel panicky. Rude Word hadn't come stumping to the door when I knocked, and I hadn't heard his barking.

A big lump came in my throat when I realised that Rude Word was dead.

"I'm sorry, Grandad," I said, trying not to cry. I meant that I was sorry for him losing his best friend, but also for me. I loved Rude Word even though I'd only met him once and he was ugly and smelly and only had three legs. And I hadn't realised I loved him until he was gone.

Grandad looked at me silently with his sad red eyes. I noticed then that there was a cardboard box by the side of the grave. Grandad bent and picked it up. He lifted it easily, and it made me

think he was stronger than he looked, or maybe Rude Word hadn't been such a fat dog after all. Or maybe that once his spirit had gone, what was left was as light as feathers and fluff.

Grandad cleared his throat, and I thought he was going to make a speech. But all he said was, "Goodbye, old friend." That was better than a long speech. When you are really sad, you can't talk about it. You just keep it inside.

And then I noticed two things. The first was that there was a face staring over the hedge from next door. It was a girl. A bit older than me. She had dark skin and long hair in a ponytail, and her face had a serious expression that was just right for a funeral.

The second thing I noticed was that Rude Word was lying in the shadows by the fence. Not lying dead but lying like a fat lazy dog that can't be bothered to get up.

"What the ...?" I started to say.

"What's up?" said Grandad.

I pointed at Rude Word.

"He's ... he's ... not dead!"

"Course he's not dead, you doylum. Why would you think he's ..." Then Grandad looked at the box in his hands. "Oh, I see."

"Who is it then?" I asked, feeling very confused.

Grandad shook his head as if it was obvious, then he opened the box and angled it towards me. There lay the wig, curled up again like a sleeping cat.

Now I really did say a bad word.

"Steady, lad," said Grandad. "No need for cussing in front of t'dog."

"But why the heck are you burying your wig?"

Then Grandad put a hand in the box and drew out the wig. He handled it gently, as if it were a puppy, or a human baby.

"It just wasn't the same after it went in the beck," Grandad said. "It lost the will to go on."

And it did look in a sorry state, limp and dirty. Grandad stroked it tenderly.

"Well, why don't you just throw it away?" I asked.

"Throw it away! Is that what you'll do with me when I'm gone? Just chuck us in the wheelie bin and have done with me?"

"No, Grandad … But couldn't you recycle it?"

"No, you can't. It's not plastic; it's real hair. Made in 1978 by the finest wigmaker in the whole North of England."

I heard a sound of stifled laughter then, and I remembered the girl at the hedge. Suddenly, I felt very embarrassed.

"Can we just get it over with?" I hissed.

"What? Oh yes, the Last Rites. Anyway, I'm burying the wig because it's organic and it'll break down into compost. So it'll give something back to the universe. Flowers will grow out of it. Circle of life. Same as *The Lion King*."

And then Grandad turned towards the hedge.

"Hey, you, little lass from next door. You any good with a spade?"

"I don't know," she said. "Never tried."

"Come on then," Grandad said. "This hole won't fill itself up. You can squeeze in that gap at the far end of the hedge."

She was there in a few seconds, so now there were three of us standing round the grave. The wig was back in its cardboard coffin. I felt a bit shy in front of the girl. I was worried in case Grandad was going to make us sing a hymn or something.

But Grandad just said, "Bye-bye then, old friend," and he placed the box in the hole. He pulled the spade out from the ground and gave it to the girl. She shovelled the loose soil over the box. I could have done it just as well. Rude Word came over to have a look.

"What's he called?" asked the girl, patting his head.

"Rude Word," I said.

The girl laughed again.

"Cool name. What about you?"

"Kyle."

There was a short silence, and then Grandad said, "Daft lad. Now you're supposed to ask her."

"Er ... yeah. What's your name?" I said.

"Karthi."

"Oh. This is Grandad."

"Hello, Grandad."

"Hello. Now we're finished with the ceremonials, me and our Kyle are gonna stroll down to the beck and have a bit of a gander. There's summat there I wanted to show him. You can come an' all if you fancy it."

"OK," said Karthi, and I groaned inside. I was looking forward to exploring with Grandad, and now it had got ... complicated.

"Grand. But go and check with your mam first," Grandad said.

Eight
Toothache

Five minutes later, the four of us were wandering over the scruffy field down to the beck.

I wasn't good with new people, so Grandad and Karthi did most of the chatting.

"When did you move in?" asked Grandad.

"Just last week," Karthi replied.

"How do you like it?"

"It's all right."

"Where did you move from?" Grandad said.

I thought that Karthi would say somewhere far away, but she said, "Chapeltown."

"Ooof," said Grandad. "That's a bit rough. It's better here."

"But I suppose you mean 'Where did we come from *originally*?' That's what people normally

want to know. And by that they normally mean, 'Why are you here?'"

"Maybe some people," said Grandad. "Maybe a lot of people. But not me. I'll be honest with you. As a rule, I don't much like anyone who doesn't come from Yorkshire. In fact, I don't much like anyone who doesn't come from Leeds. And if I'm really honest, I don't like many who comes from Leeds either. But you seem all right."

"Gee, thanks," Karthi said.

"You're welcome," Grandad replied. "Is it just you and your mam?"

"Yeah."

There was a pause, then she said in a way that sounded casual but I knew wasn't, "My dad died."

"Oh, I'm sorry, lass," Grandad said. "That's … that's shite that is."

Another pause.

"He got killed in the civil war in Sri Lanka. That's why my mum came here. I was little. Like, two or something. We were in a boat. And then travelling for a long time. I can't really remember it. Then we were here."

I felt a bit funny listening to that. I thought a lot about my own problems – all the little things that made my life not good. Hearing about much worse things happening to someone else should make you realise that your own troubles aren't that bad. But it doesn't work like that.

If you've got a toothache, and then you find out that someone's got run down by a bus, it doesn't make your toothache go away. If anything, it makes it worse. It just adds to how miserable you are. OK, maybe it might stop you whining about it, the whatever it is that's up with you, but you don't feel any better.

And then we'd reached the line of bushes and pushed through them to the beck.

"*Cooooool*," said Karthi when she saw the bubbling brown water. "I didn't even know this was here."

Just being near the beck again made me feel happy, and I really wanted Karthi to like it as much as I did.

"It doesn't look much," I said, "but there's fish called bullheads, and little baby underwater

scorpion things called crayfish. You have to hold your hand flat, like this, so they don't bite. They can take your finger off as easy as anything."

"I've got something even better to show you today, lad," said Grandad.

"What is it?" I said, dying to know. "Another fish? A big one?"

"Better than a fish. But stop talking and get walking."

Then Grandad started to plod along the path by the side of the beck.

I hung back a bit so I could talk to Karthi. I sort of wanted to and didn't at the same time.

"I'm sorry about your dad," I said. "It's really ..."

Karthi looked down, and I worried that I shouldn't have said anything. Sometimes when bad things happen you want to talk about them and sometimes you don't.

"It's fine," she said.

Before I got the chance to say something that made things worse, Grandad announced, "Here we are."

Nine

The Killer Worm

We didn't seem to be anywhere special. The beck still burbled away on one side and the scruffy old field still sloped up on the other.

I had a quick look at Karthi, trying to work out if she was bored, but she had one of those faces where you don't know what they're thinking.

There was an old rusty sheet of corrugated iron on the ground a little way from the path. Grandad walked over to it and bent down stiffly, slipping his fingers under the edge.

"OK, my slithery friends, let's see if you're still here," he said. He lifted the sheet up and moved it carefully to one side.

I let out a shout. OK, maybe a scream.

Karthi gasped.

In the dark space under the corrugated iron, the grass had died and turned yellow, but something there was definitely alive.

"SNAKES!" I yelled.

I'd never seen a snake before in real life.

For a second, all I saw was the snakes squirming, and I knew that there was more than one of them. They were brown, and about as thick as a fat finger, and as long as your arm up to your elbow. I counted: one, two, three, four.

Four snakes!

Here, in Leeds!

"Are they poisonous?" I said, kind of hoping that they were.

"Oh yes, deadly," said Grandad. "If I get bitten, you'll have to suck the poison out."

And then he went down on one knee and put his hand gently next to one of the snakes, with his knuckles nudging it. I was too stunned to even make a sound.

The snake stuck its tongue out in a very snaky way and wriggled onto Grandad's hand. I thought this was the bravest thing I'd ever seen.

Then I heard Karthi giggle.

"Not snakes – slow worms," she said. "We did them in Biology. They're a kind of lizard without any legs. And they're not even a bit poisonous."

"You're a bright lass," said Grandad with a chuckle.

I felt like a fool. Also relieved. I didn't want to have to suck the poison out if Grandad got bitten.

Karthi moved close to Grandad so she could see. "Can I have a go at holding one?"

"Aye," he said. "Just be gentle with him. If they get scared, they can shrug off their tail, which twitches and dances all by itself. It dunt do them much harm, but not much good either."

Karthi held out her hand, and Grandad let the slow worm writhe onto it. It twisted round and made her giggle.

"Now, if you look close, you can see what makes it different from a snake," Grandad said. "First, it's got eyelids, like you and me, but a snake hasn't."

And the slow worm blinked as if to demonstrate this.

"Second, see how it opens its gob a bit when it sticks its tongue out? Now, a snake has a gap in its mouth so it can poke out its tongue without opening it."

And again the slow worm did what it was supposed to do and parted its lips to stick its tongue out.

"But the way I normally tell it's a slow worm is that it's got a sort of shiny look to it," said Grandad. "Snakes don't, not unless it's a grass snake just out of the water."

"Do you get grass snakes round here too?" I asked.

"You do," Grandad replied. "They love the water. They're a bit bigger and a lovely green colour with a yellow necklace you can't miss. They're not poisonous either, but they'll give you a bite if you grab them, and that's not very nice, I can tell you. The only snake in England that's poisonous is the adder, but they don't live round here."

Then I remembered something, kind of hoping it might impress Grandad. And Karthi ...

"Snakes aren't poisonous," I said. "Poisonous is for something you eat, like poisonous mushrooms. It's venomous, not poisonous, when you talk about snakes."

"All right, clever clogs," Grandad said with a smile. "Either way, don't eat 'em!"

All the time we'd been talking, Karthi had been holding the slow worm up close to her face, studying it. Then she said, "Aw, gross! What's it doing?"

"Oh aye," said Grandad. "I meant to tell you. They only have two defences. The first, like I said, is to leave their tail behind 'em. The other is to have a poo on you."

I spotted a disgusting smear of browny-green gunk on Karthi's hand. I felt quite happy about this as I was jealous of her getting to hold the slow worm while I just stood there.

"Take it off me!" she said, sounding a bit less than cool for the first time since I'd met her.

"Give it here," said Grandad, and took the snaky lizard from her. Karthi wiped her hand on the grass, then rinsed it in the beck, then wiped it on the grass again.

"Can I have a go?" I said, thinking it was probably all pooed out by now.

"Not this chap. He's had enough excitement for one day."

Then Grandad bent and picked up another slow worm. I took it from him and felt the thrill that comes from handling a wild creature. It coiled and curled around my fingers, smooth and warm and dry. The rest of the universe disappeared, and there was just me and the slow worm in our world together.

I stared at the endless variations of browns and greys on its body. You'd normally think of brown as being a boring colour, but this wasn't "just" brown. This was a hundred different shades. I could have stayed there for ever, playing with the living brown jewel. It didn't even poo on me!

"OK then, Kyle, let's put him back with his pals."

I kneeled and let the slow worm crawl off my hand, and Grandad carefully put the corrugated iron sheet back exactly where it had been. It was as if we'd never seen this miracle, this world of the slow worms.

Ten

No Trespassing!

"That was actually pretty amazing," said Karthi as we stood by the beck.

Grandad gave a satisfied grunt. Then he said, "Aye, nature's better than owt. Better than telly. Better than that internet you have. Nature's fish and chips for the soul. And it can look after itself, mostly. It's only us lot that messes things up."

Then Grandad's face changed.

"And I'm going to show you summat that's a prime example of us messing things up," he said. "Follow me."

Grandad set off again along the path by the beck, with Karthi, me and Rude Word following.

After a few minutes, I sensed that something about Grandad had changed. He was jabbing his

stick into the ground with each step, and his back
looked hunched and stiff. I knew he was old, but
sometimes I'd forget it because his mind was
always zipping about and I never knew what he
was going to say next. But now he began to look
like an old man.

"Where we going?" asked Karthi when we'd
gone a bit further.

"You'll see," said Grandad a bit grumpily.

Karthi gave me a shrug that said "What's up
with him?" I gave her an "I don't know" shrug back.

The beck and the land around it slowly
changed as we walked. We left the estates of
red-brick houses behind us, and the beck here was
overgrown with bigger bushes and trees.

Grandad had walked further down the trail,
and I ran to catch up with him. Then I saw that
he'd stopped dead.

"This is what I brought you to see," he said.

The banks of the beck were steeper here, so
that the water was down a metre or so below us.
Its flow was faster, so the green-brown water was

frothy and frantic. And trees overhung it, almost hiding the clouds above.

But that wasn't what Grandad wanted us to see. The path was blocked here with rows of barbed wire that went right down to the water and then bent back along the bank so you couldn't reach the beck at all. I looked over to the other side of the beck, and it was the same there: barbed wire was cutting off any way of getting to the water. There was a sign on the barbed wire. I moved closer so I could read what it said:

KEEP OUT
PRIVATE PROPERTY
DANGER
CONSTRUCTION WORK

Underneath that, it said in smaller writing:

Trespassers WILL be prosecuted.

And then in even smaller writing:

This land is the property of XLS Construction and Development Limited.

Eleven

The Cunning Plan

"What does it mean?" Karthi said. She had moved closer to the sign too, right next to me – close enough that I felt her hair brush my arm.

"What it means, lass, is that these here bog-rats are building a warehouse and a car park a bit further down the beck. There's no blinking need for it. Plenty of waste ground around here they could use instead."

"Does that matter much?" I asked. "I mean, they won't build it on the beck, will they?"

"No, but they're going to do all kinds of things that will ruin it," Grandad said. "They don't want the car park flooding, so they're going to build steep concrete banks. And cut back all the trees. And they'll stop folk like us rambling along here."

"What's so bad about concrete banks?" I wondered aloud.

Grandad turned on me in a rage.

"Because for the first time since I were a lad, we've got water voles along here. And they live in tunnels on the bank. How's a vole supposed to tunnel into a concrete bank? I think your head's made of concrete if you can't see that."

"I don't think Kyle meant anything by it," said Karthi.

"Aye, well, happen you're right," Grandad said. "I get a bit worked up about this."

"Haven't people complained and tried to stop it?" asked Karthi.

"Too right they have. Letters to the council, letters to the MP. But these big companies have lawyers who earn more in a day pushing a pen around than I used to earn in a year digging bloody coal up from the ground."

"So there's nothing we can do about it?" said Karthi. "My mum always says, if you don't like something, change it; and if you can't change it, put up with it."

I looked at Grandad and saw that his face had shifted again. In place of the grumpiness, I saw a sort of sly pleasure.

"Your mam's a wise lady," he said to Karthi. "I can't help getting old. I can't help dying. I can't help that Leeds United got relegated. But there is something I can do about this."

I could tell that this was something exciting from the energy that seemed to pulse in his wiry arms and legs and made his nose hairs vibrate.

"What is it, Grandad?" I asked.

"Right, well, before you can build stuff, you've got to make sure there's no rare beasts and flowers and whatnot on the site. It's the law, that is. No way round it. Now, this lot of wazzocks have owned this stretch for years, and they've made sure there's nothing much of interest left. So, when the council comes to check it out next week, there'll be no reason not to let the building work go ahead, especially when they've been wined and dined by the men in suits. But you go a couple of miles back up the way we came, and there's a little

colony of something very rare. You know what they are, don't you?"

"The crayfish!" I said.

"Aye, got it in one."

"I know what you're gonna do," I said. And then I started to laugh. A giggle at first, but then a full-on belly laugh. Grandad smiled, showing the unnatural whiteness of his false teeth.

"What are you two on about?" said Karthi.

"You tell her, Kyle."

"I told you about the crayfish?" I said. "Well, they're protected. So Grandad's going to take some from where they live and put them in this part of the beck, where these inspectors will find them. Then they won't be able to build the warehouse. Genius."

"Er, hang on, lad, I never said any of that," Grandad added. "It wouldn't exactly be a hundred per cent legal. So you don't know anything about this scheme, OK?"

"But we want to help!" I said. I looked at Karthi, hoping she'd be on my side.

"No, now wait. It's OK for an old codger like me to bend the rules a bit. If I get collared, I don't mind having my day in court. I've had my fun, and I don't mind spending a year or two behind bars as long as the food's OK and they have the *Yorkshire Post* in the prison library. But youngsters like you two don't need that on your record. Nay, I'll carry that weight."

"We'll take the chance, won't we?" I said, looking at Karthi again.

"Er, I want to be a lawyer when I grow up, so maybe not," Karthi said.

"Smart lass," said Grandad.

Twelve

Bumface and Dried Bogey

Rude Word had been sitting there quietly, minding his own business, but then he started to bark. I saw a flash of yellow, and two guys appeared wearing yellow hi-vis jackets over dark blue uniforms. They looked like the police. Or, rather, they looked like people trying to look like the police.

"Can we help you?" said one unhelpfully.

He had a huge, bum-like face, with all his features crammed into the middle of it. His peaked cap looked too small for him, perched on top of his head.

The other one was small and wiry, and looked like a dried bogey come to life. He held a lead, and a big dog strained at the end of it. It looked like an Alsatian crossed with a Tasmanian devil.

You could see it wanted to be involved in some mayhem – tearing out throats, ripping off faces, that sort of thing.

I took a step back. The dog began to growl when it saw Rude Word, and a big line of drool went all the way from its jaws to the ground. Rude Word ignored it and just carried on sniffing and weeing.

"Help me?" said Grandad. "Aye, maybe you can. Me dog here has lost his leg, and we're out looking for it. So if you could just check in them bushes for it, that'd be grand."

"I think you know very well what I mean, sir," said Bumface. "This is private property, and you'll be committing a criminal offence if you trespass on it."

"Two things, young man," said Grandad. "One, trespass is not a criminal offence. Two, I'm not trespassing." Then he put his rough old hand through the barbed wire and said, "Oh yes I am." Then took it out again and said, "Oh no I'm not."

That made me laugh.

"That's a bit childish," said Bumface.

"So is dressing up in fancy costumes like you two bozos are doing," said Grandad. "Anyway, we were just going. But if I can jot down your names, I'll be writing to your employer, the *Yorkshire Post* and my MP about your conduct. Parading around, trying to stop normal folk out with their dog. Do you know what that is? Fascism. And don't say you were just obeying orders. That's what all fascists say. Apart from Hitler, because he was giving the orders. I fought against your lot in the war. Wouldn't have it then, and I won't have it now."

"Oh, clear off, you miserable old git," said Dried Bogey. But the two of them were walking away, dragging their hellhound with them. They clearly didn't want to get further tangled up with Grandad, for which you couldn't really blame them.

"That's right," said Grandad. "Retreat like you did in North Africa when us Desert Rats gave you a bit of the old bayonet."

"Nutter," shouted Dried Bogey.

"Is that the best you can do?" Grandad called back. "Me dog here can do better than that, and he's not even bright for a dog."

Dried Bogey stood there trying to think of a comeback, but in the end just shouted "Nutter" again, which made Grandad's point for him.

"If you two got hanged for beauty, you'd die innocent," was the last thing that Grandad said to them. It took a second for Karthi and me to get it, but then we burst out laughing, and so did Rude Word.

"What was that rubbish you said about the war and the Germans?" said Karthi, still giggling as we walked away. "I know you're old, but not that old."

"Well, lass," said Grandad. "It's wrong to tell lies apart from on very specific occasions, such as when defeating evil Nazis. Or when that tight git Potto from the pub wants to borrow a tenner and you tell him you're skint."

"But was the rest of it true?" I asked. "About it not being a criminal offence if you trespass?"

"Aye, I think so," Grandad said. "It's complicated. They keep the law dense and knotty so that normal folk can't figure it out. We'll have to wait till Karthi here gets her wig and gown and the little wooden hammer, and then she'll tell us."

I tried to get more info about Grandad's great plan out of him on the way back. But all he would say was that "Preparations are underway" and that it had to be done just before the next environmental investigation on 21st May.

That was exactly a week away.

*

When we got back, Karthi's mum was standing by the fence, waiting for us. She looked just like Karthi but old. I mean mum-aged – not old like Grandad.

"Hope she wasn't any trouble," Karthi's mum said.

"Trouble? No trouble at all," Grandad replied. "She's champion. Going to be the Lord High Chancellor one day."

Thirteen

Home Life

All week, I was thinking about Grandad's plan. The last thing he'd said to me was "Don't tell your mam and dad. It's not their sort of thing."

I wouldn't have told them anyway. I don't tell my mum and dad things. Who does? Most of the stuff you don't tell them is sort of sad or just in some way not good, so why would you? If bad things happen, you should just keep them on the inside, where they can't do any harm.

Our estate isn't like Grandad's. There aren't any broken windows or burnt-out cars. The front gardens are nice and neat, with flowers and, er, shrubs, if that's the word. Two of the houses have artificial grass, which glows with a kind

of chemical intensity, like a Haribo, and never
needs mowing.

We moved here a couple of years ago, and
I haven't made many local friends. Well, *any*
local friends. There are kids around, but they're
all either toddlers playing on those trainer
bikes without pedals, or older teenagers who'd
rather eat their own sick than hang out with a
thirteen-year-old like me.

Mum and Dad both work really hard, and I'm
usually on my own when I get back from school.
I don't mean to play a sad song on my tiny violin.
It's fine. I like being on my own, most of the time.

I know I said that I don't tell my parents stuff,
but the weird thing is that I know they'd like it if
I did. Especially my dad. Maybe he could tell that
things weren't amazing at school. That bad stuff
was happening there. Maybe he could have helped.
But sometimes it's hard to talk about things. To
tell people that you're, er, you know, sad.

I thought my parents were sad too. And I
thought I knew why. I was pretty sure that the

"appointments" they were going to in town were at Leeds hospital.

There was something wrong with my mum.

Fourteen
Plan 2

If Grandad had a plan, then so did I. He'd said I couldn't get involved with the scheme to release the crayfish, but if I just turned up at his house when he was about to go on the mission, then he'd have to take me. And even if Grandad didn't take me, I could just follow him. What was he going to do – call the police?

But how could I find out when Grandad was going to strike? I knew it could be any time before the inspection on the 21st. I thought this over, then had an idea.

On Wednesday night after tea, I said to my dad, "I left a schoolbook at Grandad's last week, and I need to go and pick it up."

Dad gave me a funny look but said, "Fine. I'll run you over there. Or you can get the bus."

Now it was time for the cunning part of my plan.

"No," I said. "You see, when I was last there, Grandad said he had various important things to do. Very important things. I don't want to go there when he's busy. So can you find out from him when I can't go? Then I'll go some other time."

I knew Grandad didn't have any important things to do apart from The Plan. So whenever Grandad told Dad I couldn't go, that was when I'd go. I said it was cunning!

"I'll give him a call later on," said Dad. Then he added, "It's nice you're getting on well with him. He's been lonely since your granny died. But ... are you sure it's all, I don't know, OK?"

"It is, yeah," I replied.

"OK," Dad said, looking a bit confused. "And what do you do while you're there?"

"We explore. Down by the beck mainly. I told you about the crayfish and the slow worms. I didn't think animals like that lived around here. Grandad makes it exciting."

Dad smiled, and you could see in his eyes he was thinking back to when he was a boy.

"He was always an eccentric old feller, your grandad," Dad said. "I was a bit embarrassed about him when I was your age. I wanted a dad like all the other kids, not one who was an Elvis impersonator at weekends. And he left school at fifteen, so most of what's in his head, he put there himself. Anyway, like I said, I'm glad. As long as you say you're happy with it all. And last time I called him, Grandad said you were getting on OK with the girl who lives next door ..."

Time for a change of subject.

"When's your next appointment in town?" I asked.

Dad looked thoughtful for a moment, as if it was time to tell me what was going on. But then he just said, "Not till next week. Wednesday. It's an important one. We'll be ... getting results."

Then I went to my room, saying I had homework to do. It was true but also a way of escaping any more questioning about Karthi.

Later on, Dad shouted up the stairs, "Grandad says you can go round any time except Saturday morning, when he's getting his ears syringed at the doctors."

Bingo.

Fifteen

On the Bus

I got the bus to Grandad's on Saturday morning. It was good getting the bus. Your fate wasn't in your hands while you were sitting there. It was someone else's job to get you where you were going, and you could just let your mind wander. Or you could read a book.

And you were safe.

Or maybe not.

"Oh look, it's Wilson, with his nose in a book," said a voice. "Sweet, eh?"

I knew something was wrong even before he spoke. Something about the air. Something changed.

I didn't want to look up.

I looked up.

It was Dredge.

And two of his mates. One called Bullet, because of his skinhead. The other was called Whetstone. This was as bad as it could be. These kids were the worst. The ones who made life at school hell.

The weird thing was that they weren't that thick. Dredge was in the top set for most things. Whetstone was middling. Bullet was ... OK, Bullet was pretty thick. Sometimes at school they'd seem all right – they'd joke and mess about, nothing too bad. And then for no good reason they'd turn.

Things were OK at the beginning of Year Eight. All right, so I wasn't the most popular kid in the year, but I had people to talk to. Then, one break-time, I was standing around with some other kids from my form. Dredge and his mates were a few metres away, and he was sitting on one of the concrete benches that lined the yard. I'd noticed that there was a giant dollop of sloppy bird poo on the edge of the bench. I'd been thinking that you wouldn't want to sit in it. Then the bell went for the end of break, and Dredge stood up. As he did, he put his hand in the bird poo.

Dredge said a bad word but sort of laughed at the same time. And his mates laughed too, as any normal person would. Bird poo. Not exactly a tragedy. And I laughed. I'd seen the whole thing coming – the build-up, the event, the laughter. It was all harmless.

Then Dredge saw me. He laughed again, but it was a different kind of laugh – harder, forced.

"*Hah. Hah. Hah.*"

And then Dredge stopped laughing, and the others did too, and for a second I laughed alone.

"What you laughing at?" said Dredge, his smile dying.

I still didn't realise the danger. But I knew things had changed. Dredge had moved closer. He was a cool kid. And he had good hair. Sort of floppy but like it was radio-controlled, like a drone so it always flopped in the right way.

"Nothing," I said.

Everyone was watching now.

"Really? Nothing?" said Dredge. "You laugh at nothing, do you? Are you mental?"

"No. It was just ... when you put your hand in—"

Without warning, Dredge said, "Laugh at this," and slapped me with the hand that he'd put in the bird poo. It wasn't a hard slap. Not the kind that made a crack like a whip. It was almost friendly. And because it wasn't hard, his hand stayed in contact with my cheek, and he pressed the bird poo into my face.

People went "*Ewwww*", gasped, spluttered, laughed. Most of them didn't even know who I was until then. But now I'd come into focus for them. I was a kid with bird poo on his face.

"Aw, don't cry," said Dredge.

Was I crying? The world was a bit blurry, so maybe I was. And he put his hand to my hair and wiped the rest of the bird shit into it.

The crowd clearly thought this was even funnier. They were still guffawing as they went into class.

I went straight to the toilets and tried to wash the filth off me. When I arrived late to my class, everyone jeered. Mr Pool, the Maths teacher, gave me a detention.

So that was when it all changed for me. From then on, I found that at break and lunchtime there

never seemed to be anyone for me to hang out with. The kids who'd been my friends became just kids I knew. I was the Birdshit Boy.

Weirdly, no one seemed to blame Dredge for this. People thought it was me that had started it by laughing. Maybe it was because of the way Dredge had taken his revenge – not battering me but humiliating me. It would have been better for me if he had properly hit me and his friends had joined in. I would have been an innocent victim and not just the loser I was. A joke.

People always say you should go to the teachers about this kind of thing. But I imagined how pathetic it would sound. "Sir, that boy wiped some bird poo on my face."

No thanks.

So then it was just me.

Alone.

"Let's have a look then," said Dredge now, on the bus. His voice was bright, teeth white, his eyes shining with fake friendliness.

He was kneeling on the seat in front of me, facing backward. Bullet was next to him, Whetstone across the aisle. There was no one else on the top deck of the bus. That was bad.

Then Dredge leaned over and took my book out of my hands. If I'd held on to it properly, that would have been good, making him fight for it. If I'd just let him take it without resisting at all, that would have been good too. But I held on to it just enough to mean Dredge had to give it a little tug before he got it. That was bad. I'd shown pointless resistance.

"Don't worry," he said, "I'll look after it. *The Lord of the Rings*, excellent choice, great book."

Just for a second, I thought that maybe Dredge was a Tolkien fan and that this was going to be all right after all.

A teacher had given me the book in Year Five. I'd been too young for it, and it'd taken me two years to finish it. But then I read it over and over again, and now the cover was creased like Grandad's face, and the pages were brown, the edges worn smooth and soft. I'd read other books

too, but I always came back to it. In my head, I
lived in Middle Earth, where if you were brave,
even the little people could defeat evil.

"Give it here," said Bullet, trying to take the
book from Dredge.

"Don't snatch!" said Dredge, in a voice like a
teacher. "Ask nicely."

"Please, sir, can I have a go on it?" said Bullet,
in a wimpy voice that I guessed was meant to
sound like me.

Dredge let the book drop into Bullet's hands.

Bullet opened the book to a random page and
pretended to read it for a few seconds. Then he
stuck his stubby finger up his nose. He pulled his
finger out again, examined it carefully and then
wiped it on the page.

Whetstone laughed, and Dredge said, "That was
unkind, Bullet. Give the nice boy his book back."

Bullet chucked the book at me, bouncing it off
my chest.

"Anyway, this is our stop," said Dredge. "Nice
chatting. See you at school."

I hadn't spoken a word yet. But now I said in a sort of hard mumble, "Dirty dog." I wished it had been something better. More cutting. Funnier. Anything.

They found it funny. Bullet and Whetstone burst out laughing, and Dredge leaned over and ruffled my hair, like you would do to a friend. Then they were up and swinging their way down the aisle.

At my stop, I looked at the book next to me on the seat. The red Eye of Sauron stared at me. We had been together all these years. It was ruined now. I got up and left it on the seat.

Sixteen

Terrible Discovery

I walked from the bus stop to Grandad's feeling weird and empty, like I wasn't fully in my body. Not looking down on myself or anything like that. More like when you were a little kid and you were colouring in and you tried really hard to stay inside the lines but you always went over.

I knew that I should feel some things. I should have been furious with Dredge and his gormless sidekicks. I should have been sorry that I'd lost one of the things I loved most in the world. I should have been embarrassed about how rubbish I was at dealing with it. I should have smashed Dredge in his smiling face, even if it meant taking a beating from the three of them.

But I didn't feel anything. There was just this fog. A grey nothing. And I walked in it not seeing, not hearing, not feeling. Was this what death was like?

When I got to Grandad's house, I remembered why I was there, and the fog cleared. I was there to help him on his mission. We were superheroes, fighting against evil forces for all that was right.

I banged at the door and waited to hear Rude Word's thudding steps. And as I waited, I thought about my speech. I was going to say that I understood why Grandad didn't want me to get involved, but that it was the responsibility of the young to protect the planet, like Greta whatshername. And if I had to go to jail to save the beck and all its animals, then I would.

I couldn't hear anything from inside the house.

My heart fell. Grandad must have already set out on the mission. But then I thought I could easily catch up with him. He could only have gone one way. Grandad's house was attached to Karthi's on one side, but on the other there was a

gap where you could get to the back garden. From there, I could easily run down to the beck.

When I was in the back garden, I thought I might as well bang on the back door, just in case Grandad was inside and hadn't heard me. The back door had that kind of wobbly glass in it that you can't see through, or not clearly anyway. I gave the glass a rap with my hand, not expecting anything.

And then I saw something. A movement, low down.

Rude Word?

Must have been.

I knocked again, peering through the glass, straining to see. I could see there was a dark shape on the floor. And I thought I heard a noise. A sort of whine. And then after that, a bark. Not a normal Rude Word kind of bark, which was hungry or grumpy. This sounded almost sad.

"Grandad! Grandad!" I yelled, suddenly full of fear.

"What is it?" came a voice.

I turned, and there was Karthi, looming over the hedge like when I'd first seen her.

"It's Grandad," I said. "I think he might be ..."

"He never locks the door," Karthi said. "Just open it."

I turned the handle, and the door opened into the kitchen.

Grandad was lying face down on the floor. Rude Word was next to him, his big head resting on Grandad's back.

I crouched down and turned Grandad over. His eyes were closed. I was relieved, in a way. Sometimes in films, when they want to show someone's dead, they have their eyes wide open, staring blindly. Eyes like that can only mean you're dead. But closed eyes can mean anything.

"Grandad! Grandad!" I said again. And then, "Wake up," which was silly, as if he'd overslept and I was bringing him a cup of tea in the morning.

"I'm calling an ambulance," Karthi said behind me.

She must have slipped through the gap in the hedge and followed me inside.

It was like her. Being practical. Not
screaming, not standing there like a dummy but
doing something useful.

Grandad's face looked so grey it was almost
blue. I couldn't tell if he was breathing. I tried to
remember what you were supposed to do. Kiss of
life? The thing where you pound down on their
chest? My head was all muddled, and all I could do
was keep on saying, "Grandad, Grandad."

I heard Karthi on the phone, asking for an
ambulance, giving them Grandad's address. Then
she handed the phone to me and said, "I'm getting
me mum."

I put her phone to my ear.

"Hello, hello, is that the grandson?" said the
person on the line.

I didn't understand how the woman on the
phone would know that, but then I realised Karthi
must have told her.

"Yes," I said.

"Tell me, love, is your grandad conscious? Is he
awake?"

"I don't think so."

"Can you tell if he's breathing?" the woman asked. "This is very important ..."

"I don't know."

"Put your hand on his chest. Can you feel it moving at all?"

I placed my hand over Grandad's heart.

"I think so," I said. "A bit."

I was very close to crying.

"That's OK, love," the lady told me. "You're doing great. Will you speak to him for me? Will you speak clearly in his ear?"

"What shall I say?"

"Just ask him if he can hear you."

I leaned close to Grandad's ear and almost shouted, "Grandad, can you hear me?"

Rude Word had been sitting next to Grandad the whole time, staring into his old face. Now he gave another of his yowling yelps.

"Was that your grandad?" said the lady on the phone.

"No, it was Rude ... I mean it was his dog. He's got three legs."

Then the lady said, "Has he got any obstruction in his airway? Anything in his mouth?"

I thought about Grandad's false teeth.

"He might have his teeth in," I said. "Do I have to take them out?"

"Only if they're broken or if they've fallen back in his throat. Can you check?"

I put my finger up to Grandad's lips and tried to feel if his teeth were there.

And then Grandad's eyes opened, and he said, "Geroff."

"Grandad!" I said. "I thought ..."

If I'd been hoping that Grandad was going to suddenly spring back to life, I was wrong. His eyes half closed, then closed fully. I remembered the lady on the phone.

"He spoke," I told her. "He's not dead."

"You've done great, love. The ambulance will be with you in a couple of minutes. You just hold on. Both of you."

Then Karthi was back with her mum. That was good. It was time for the grown-ups to take

charge. Karthi's mum kneeled beside me and took Grandad's hand.

"Paddy," she said, "it's Manisha from next door. You're OK. The ambulance is coming."

Paddy.

I never thought of Grandad as having a first name. It was like finding out that God had a first name. Kevin. Kevin God. Unless God was his first name, and it was God something. God Sidebottom or whatever.

Then Karthi's mum said to me, "You better call your mum and dad. Tell them what's happened."

I nodded.

My fingers were like sausages when I tried to dial.

Dad answered.

"Dad, it's Grandad," I said. "He's not well. He's ..."

I tried to explain. I'd got halfway through when the ambulance people were there in green uniforms. It was a blur after that, and I can't really remember what went on, except that they said I could ride in the ambulance. Somehow my

parents had got the message about which hospital, and they were going to meet us there.

As I was getting in the ambulance, I remembered Rude Word.

"The dog ..." I said to Karthi.

"We'll take care of Rude Word," she said, "till your grandad's back home."

Seventeen

Last Words

I sat in the ambulance as it drove to the hospital. If things were different, I might have enjoyed it. All the gadgets and gizmos in the back, the calm ambulance people doing their thing, the sense of travelling at great speed with the siren blaring.

Except Grandad was lying there, as pale as death, an oxygen mask on his face. He opened his eyes a couple more times, and he saw me and moved his hand toward me.

"Take his hand, son," one of the ambulance guys said to me.

I did, and gave it a gentle squeeze.

Grandad closed his eyes again. I kept thinking that it might be for the last time, and there was a lump in my throat. You hear that expression and

it means nothing until you feel it for yourself, and it's there, like a real thing – a rock or a piece of wood, right in your throat – and you can't swallow.

And somehow I thought that while the ambulance people were doing all the important things to keep Grandad alive, I also had a part to play. That I had to make him live by concentrating really hard.

Then I felt Grandad squeeze my hand back, and his eyes opened again. His lips moved, but I couldn't hear what he was saying. I bent my head closer, till my ear was almost touching his lips.

I heard what he said, and I understood.

Eighteen

Hospital

I didn't know what to do with myself in the A&E waiting room, with sick people and doctors and nurses and other randoms wandering around. And the plastic chairs were really uncomfortable. I couldn't sit still and kept sliding down and shifting from side to side. I thought someone might come and tell me what they were doing with Grandad, but nobody did. After a while, I went to the reception desk and asked them.

"I came in with my grandad. Mr Wilson. Is he OK?"

The woman on the desk stared at me through her thick glasses.

"He's being looked after," she said. And then she looked at the person behind me in the queue.

My mum and dad turned up soon after that, and at last I knew that I could pass it on – the burden of being sort of in charge. Not that I'd really been in charge or made any decisions, but in charge of the worrying.

Mum hugged me, and Dad went to find out what was happening. It all gets a bit fuzzy again after that, but it ended with Mum driving me home and Dad staying at the hospital.

One thing stayed clear to me during it all.

What Grandad had said.

What he'd said was, "Shed."

Nineteen

Decisions

Dad came back late that night. I'd stayed up with Mum, waiting to find out what the news was. We'd watched a movie together while we waited. I can't even remember what it was.

Dad looked shattered. Not just tired but old. Suddenly, he almost looked like Grandad.

"How is he?" asked Mum.

She always used to complain about Grandad, or joke about him. But I think underneath it she liked him really.

"Hanging in there," Dad said. "He's a tough old so-and-so."

"What is it that's up with him?" I asked.

"He had a little stroke. Well, it wasn't that little ... Plus, when he fell, he banged his head."

I didn't really know what a stroke was. But I knew it wasn't good.

"But he's going to be all right?" I asked.

"If you hadn't gone round when you did and found him, well, it wouldn't have been good."

"But he'll get better?" I said.

Dad didn't say anything. Mum gave him a hug.

And that hug … well, it made me remember the appointments Mum had been going to in town, and how she always looked like she'd been crying when she came back. And I realised that the hug was doing lots of jobs. Mum was hugging Dad for Grandad. Dad was hugging Mum for Mum.

That was how I left them, hugging, as I went to bed.

*

I knew what I had to do.

The scientists were coming to check out the site on Monday, which meant I was going to have to undertake the mission tomorrow – Sunday.

My plan was to set off early, do the deed, then go to the hospital to tell Grandad all about it. I convinced myself that giving him this good news might be the difference between him living and dying.

At breakfast, I was quiet. Mum and Dad thought it was because I was worried about Grandad, which wasn't untrue. They both made the sorts of noises you'd expect – reassuring me but also kind of preparing me for the worst. They were going to see him later on and asked if I'd like to come.

"Yes ... er, no," I said. "I need to do something first."

"What's that, love?" asked Mum.

I had to think fast.

"I need to go and check up on Rude Word. Karthi and her mum are looking after him. I want to make sure he's OK. Then I can go and tell Grandad so he won't have to worry."

Mum and Dad looked at each other. I suppose they were thinking that it was a bit odd to worry about a silly dog in these circumstances. But

maybe they also thought it was because I was afraid to visit Grandad in case the news was bad.

"OK then, son," Dad said. "We can pop in on the way."

"If you just drop me at Grandad's, I'll get the bus the rest of the way to the hospital," I said.

They glanced at each other again. I tried to look lost and sad and a bit tragic. It actually wasn't that hard as I was feeling all of those things.

Twenty

Prep

An hour later, I got out of the car and went towards Karthi's house. I bent to tie my shoelaces, giving Mum and Dad time to drive away. I'd thought about really calling in to see Rude Word, but I'd decided against it. I didn't want Karthi to think I was pressurising her to come on the mission. Not when she'd already made it clear she didn't want to as it would ruin her brilliant legal career. That sounded a bit sarky, and I probably was feeling like that.

I slipped down the side of Grandad's house and into the back garden. The house felt different. Since Granny had died, the house had got more and more scruffy with all the junk Grandad collected.

But it had always felt alive, that it had a soul. Now it was just a shell.

But Grandad's shed was still his shed. I remembered sneaking into it as a little kid. It was weirdly exciting, full of dangerous things. I dragged the door open. Inside, there was a strong smell of oil and dust and damp that I remembered. The sunlight from the doorway shone on the cobwebs strung between the tools that hung like skeletons from a rack in the ceiling. And I thought I heard something scratch and scurry in a dark corner.

Not uncreepy.

But I was here for the mission.

There was a wooden workbench along one wall. Other tools were scattered across it. A hammer. Some pliers. A pair of broken spectacles. A notebook. And there: a rectangular ice-cream tub. The tub was semi-transparent, and I could see that it was half full of water. And there were dark shapes in it.

The crayfish!

I held the box up to the light coming through the door. Yes, there they were – claws and tails, maybe half a dozen of them. Not moving. Which made the mission all the more urgent. They'd been out of their natural habitat for a couple of days. I had to act fast.

I looked around the shed in case there was anything useful for the mission in there. I wondered if Grandad might have a Samurai sword, or a crossbow, or an Amazonian blowpipe he'd collected on his travels.

There wasn't a blowpipe, or a crossbow or a sword. There was a garden rake. Nobody likes to be raked in a combat scenario. But also, nobody wants to carry a garden rake when on a mission.

I was about to go when I spotted a pair of Grandad's wellies in the corner near the door. There was a part of the plan I hadn't worked out fully: that barbed wire and how to get past it. I'd imagined somehow staying right on the edge of the beck, either keeping to the dry bits or maybe just getting my trainers a bit wet. But now I thought about it, the steep banks meant I'd be pretty much

in the water most of the time. Conditions made
for wellies!

So I grabbed Grandad's wellies and brought
them outside into the light. They were size ten,
and I was only an eight, but that didn't matter.
You can wear wellies that are too big for you. You
rattle around in them, but that's better than them
being too tight.

I turned the wellies upside down and gave them
a shake. And good job I did because one big spider,
three earwigs and a black beetle came tumbling
out. I took my trainers off and pulled the wellies
on. Now the mission could finally get underway.

Twenty-One

Phase 1

It felt very strange walking down to the beck without Grandad and Rude Word. And Karthi. But wearing Grandad's wellies made it feel like he was kind of with me.

I pushed past the bushes and found the path. On my previous trips, I hadn't realised quite how much the beck curved this way and that. With the pressure on me to fulfil the mission, I got frustrated about each bend that seemed to take me further away from my destination. And the other thing was that I couldn't see what was coming up because of the trees and bushes. Behind each bend, a security guard might have been lurking with a fierce dog.

With all of my focus on the path ahead, I was vulnerable to an attack from behind. Which was exactly what happened.

"You are a very annoying kid."

I spun round and stared into the face of Karthi. And, lower down, Rude Word.

"Oh, hello," I said, as if I were just on a normal stroll.

"I know what you're doing," Karthi said. Her face was oddly blank, which I took to mean she was angry.

Very angry.

But Rude Word was pleased to see me. He stumped over and gave me a friendly sniff. I reached down with one hand and stroked his nose.

"You might at least have come to say hello and tell us how your grandad's doing," Karthi said.

"Sorry. Grandad's ... well, I don't know. He isn't ... It's just that I had to finish his plan. I'm going to do this and then go to the hospital to tell him about it, and that will help him get better."

The last bit sounded very childish, even to me. And the lump in my throat decided to come back.

"Anyway," I added, "you said you didn't want to come on the mission because it would stop you becoming Lord High Chancellor."

"I just said 'lawyer'," Karthi replied. "Anyway, I've thought about it, and I can come with you as far as the 'Private Property' sign. Until then, we're just on a walk. And that's not against the law."

"OK," I said.

I had mixed feelings about this development. I was quite glad to have some help, but I'd also told myself that a solo mission was the most heroic kind, and I didn't want Karthi getting half the praise.

Also, I'd only ever hung out with Karthi when Grandad was there, and I didn't really know how I should act without him.

So, anyway, I carried on walking along the winding path, still holding the ice-cream tub, still feeling excited about the mission, still worried about Grandad. But now I was also nervous about what to say to Karthi to stop her thinking I was a doofus.

And then suddenly things got about a million per cent worse.

Twenty-Two

Level 1 Boss

I pushed through some overhanging willow branches and saw three backs right in front of me. I knew right away who they were because the thing you least want to happen nearly always happens.

It was my nemesis.

Dredge.

Well, nemeses, as Whetstone and Bullet were there too.

For a second, I didn't understand what they were doing.

And then I did.

They were peeing in the beck. Not near it, as any half-decent human would do, but actually in it, polluting the natural world.

Dredge must have heard me, as he glanced backward. For a second, he looked a bit flustered, and they finished weeing and hurriedly did their trousers up.

Without thinking, I said, "That's a filthy thing to do. Animals live in there. How would you like it if someone came and peed in your house?" And then I realised that of course people peed in houses all the time – in their toilets. So I added, to clarify, "All over your carpet I mean? And your bed."

It was the longest speech I'd ever made to them.

They'd all turned round now, and Dredge was getting his composure back. I suddenly realised that this was not a great situation to be in. Then Dredge looked past me as Karthi pushed through the overhanging branches.

Now Dredge smiled a hideous wet smile.

"Hey, Wilson, is this your bird?" he said.

Bullet and Whetstone guffawed as if the idea of me having a girlfriend was the greatest joke in history.

Karthi stared right back at Dredge and the other two, and the hardness of her stare stopped

their laughter dead in its tracks. I looked at her and felt a great wave of … admiration. Karthi was like some Greek god. Hard and unstoppable and wise and strong.

Then she said, "Yeah, she is."

And then Karthi did the weirdest, most amazing thing.

She put her hand through my arm near my elbow and gave me a kiss on the cheek.

"Jealous?" she said.

Dredge stared at this little act with his gob literally hanging open.

Then poor old Rude Word came limping along the path and the three of them burst out laughing again.

That was when Dredge made his first big mistake.

"Ugliest dog I've ever seen," he said. "And the three-legged mutt isn't pretty neither."

It took his mates a second or two to get it, but then they spluttered into laughter again.

This was terrible. Dredge had said a horrible thing about Karthi. She wasn't my real girlfriend,

but I still felt I had to stick up for her, to do something. Otherwise, I was a swine, a cad, a coward. Everyone knew that. So I was going to have to punch Dredge. And that was going to be a disaster. I'd never punched anyone. I was going to miss, and even if I hit Dredge, it wouldn't hurt. And then he and his mates would beat the crap out of me. Which would be doubly rubbish as I'd get beaten up *and* Karthi would see it, adding some humiliation custard to the pain pudding.

I thought about just running away. The mission was the important thing, not this minor skirmish. All that mattered was getting my cargo to the destination.

Well, that was what I told myself.

Anyway, all that thinking took a couple of seconds, and that was the gap into which Karthi stepped.

Literally stepped. She took two, three steps forward and aimed a massive punch at Dredge's head.

Except she didn't.

Just about the oldest trick in the Book of Bullying is the one when they pretend to hit you, making you flinch. Then they laugh because they've made you look stupid and scared. So Karthi stopped her punch mid-swing. Dredge was already half ducking, half flinching. He stepped back. His heel went over the low mud bank of the beck. He tottered, he overbalanced, he fell arse first into the brown beck. The beck into which Dredge and his pals had just peed.

Dredge sat in the water up to his waist. The nice thing was that they'd peed into one of the almost still pools that sometimes formed in the beck – little backwaters where the water hardly flowed at all. So Dredge was bathing in urine as well as the green-brown sludge at the bottom of the beck.

Twenty-Three

Hopes are Crushed

Dredge ending up in the beck was pretty much the greatest moment of my life up until then. I wanted to hug Karthi – not in a boyfriend way but more like footballers hugging after scoring a brilliant goal.

Bullet and Whetstone looked stunned for a second, and then I thought I saw a smirk on Whetstone's face.

But then the focus was back on Dredge. He got half up but slipped back down on the slimy bed of the beck. Finally, he staggered out of the water, dripping, his face red with rage and humiliation.

I had no idea what was going to happen next, but violence was going to be part of it. It looked

like the mission to save the beck was going to end
before it had really begun.

And then came an unexpected intervention.

Rude Word had been watching everything
up to now in his usual passive way, just staring
from face to face. But when Dredge began moving
angrily towards Karthi, he was transformed into a
hellhound. Rude Word lurched forward, snarling
and barking. He was doing that thing only evil
dogs in films do, his top lip peeling up to reveal
dripping fangs.

Dredge gave a yelp, cringed and very nearly
fell back in the beck again, which would have
beaten his earlier fall as my best-ever moment.
Sadly, Dredge managed to steady himself. But
again, he looked a bit ridiculous.

"Keep that thing away from me!" Dredge
squealed, waving his hands in front of him.

His mates looked a bit embarrassed. The
point of following someone like Dredge is that
some of his glory reflects on you. But if he looks
silly, then the light that shines on you isn't gold
but, er, brown.

And they were probably scared of Rude Word, who was still snarling.

"This is boring," said Whetstone inaccurately. It was probably just his way of saying "Let's get the hell outa here before something else goes wrong."

But as the leader of their crappy gang, Dredge couldn't just accept defeat. He knew he had to do something to regain respect. And then his eyes settled on the ice-cream tub in my hands. Even I'd forgotten I was holding it.

"What's that, nerd?" Dredge said. "Your packed lunch?"

Then he stepped forward once again and slapped the container out of my hand.

It hit the ground, and the lid burst off it, spilling the water and the crayfish out on the bank.

"Aw, gross!" said Bullet. Whetstone made some kind of groaning noise. "What the heck are they? Like beetles or ... I don't even know what."

"They're crayfish," I yelped. "They're ..."

"You are a massive weirdo," said Dredge. And then he raised his foot and stomped down on the crayfish with his boot.

I was speechless. Couldn't utter a word or even make a sound. This really was the end of the plan. The end not only for the crayfish but for Grandad.

It was Karthi who spoke.

"Right, you idiot. Do you realise what you've done?"

"Am I bothered?" sneered Dredge. "Squashed some ... whatever the weirdo said they were."

"What they are, or were," said Karthi, "is white-clawed crayfish. They are protected under the Wildlife and Countryside Act of 1981. It is a criminal offence to harm them in any way."

"Boring," said Dredge.

Karthi gave him the hard stare again. "The penalty for harming a white-clawed crayfish is an unlimited fine and up to six months in prison. As you're underage, you'll probably get away with a £10,000 fine and a couple of months in a young offender unit."

That most definitely shut Dredge up.

You could see and almost hear Bullet and Whetstone thinking. They looked at Dredge, looked at each other and silently agreed to betray him.

"We didn't touch nothing," said Bullet.

"Yeah, it was him – Dredge," added Whetstone. "We weren't even with him."

Then they scuttled away along the path.

"Wait!" Dredge cried after them. "She's lying. It's bull. It's a bluff. We should smack 'em."

But the other two had gone. Dredge looked at us again, then he was off too. No doubt trying to outrun his fate as a secretly not very tough kid in a young offender unit that was full of very tough kids indeed.

And that was great. Then I looked down at my feet and the destruction of all my plans and schemes.

Karthi did a nice thing. She put her hand on my shoulder and gave it a squeeze.

"You tried your best," she said. "That's all anyone can do."

I got down on my knees to check in case any of the crayfish had managed to survive.

"But, anyway," Karthi continued, "you realise, don't you, that it was illegal for your grandad to have moved the crayfish in the first place, even if

he did it to try to save them. The Act is quite clear. Any disturbance is … Why are you laughing?"

It must have looked very odd to Karthi. There I was, kneeling in the mud, holding the dead crayfish in my fingers and laughing my head off. She probably thought that the stress of the past few minutes had sent me bonkers, but then I got control of myself.

"I should have known that Grandad would never do anything to endanger the crayfish," I said. I picked up one of the poor battered little bodies and held it out for Karthi to see. "Look!"

"What?" she said, now looking half annoyed as well as puzzled.

"They shed!" I said.

"Eh?"

"They're just shells. Or, er, exoskeletons. They're crustaceans. The shells don't grow with the crayfish. They have to shed them. That's what Grandad collected – not the actual crayfish, but their shells. Look!"

And now Karthi did look, and she saw what I'd seen. Not a crayfish but a perfect copy of one.

It had claws and a tail and even antennae, but it was empty.

Karthi shook her head. And then she laughed too.

Twenty-Four
Phase 2

I put the exoskeletons back in the ice-cream tub and then said, "So you're coming?"

"Not all the way, no," Karthi replied. "Even if you're not smuggling live crayfish, you're still going to be trespassing, which is against the law. Anyway, I've got to look after Rude Word. He can hardly go wading through rivers, not when he's only got three legs. But I'll come as far as the sign. After that, you're on your own."

"Fine," I said in a resigned sort of way. "But thanks. You know, for helping. With Dredge and his cronies. You were ... amazing."

Karthi looked a bit bashful then, and smiled and glanced down. "I hate bullies," she said. "They ruin everything."

Then we started walking along the path, and I felt the happiest I'd felt since Grandad had got sick.

But one thing was on my mind. I started talking, hoping that the right words would come out.

"The ... thing you said. When you said that, um, thing. Back there. And you, er, did that thing. Um, that was, I mean, did you, what I'm trying to say is ..."

Rude Word shook his head at my bumbled speech.

"Do I want to go out with you?" Karthi said.

"Er ..."

"Is that what you're trying to say?" she went on.

"No. Yes. I don't know."

Karthi stopped and gave me a stare. Not her now famous hard stare. But also not a soft stare. As stares go, it was a medium one. But I had no idea what it meant.

"I think you're OK, and I quite like hanging out with you," Karthi said. "If I wanted a boyfriend, I wouldn't definitely not go out with you, but I don't want one, so no. OK?"

Once I'd worked out what she was saying, that
was actually fine, and I breathed a sigh of relief.

"OK," I said. "Anyway, thanks for pretending."

"You're welcome. And by the way ..."

"What?"

"Nice wellies."

So we carried on, with everything now a bit
clearer. I was going to have to complete the
mission alone. And I didn't have a girlfriend.

It took us half an hour to reach the "Private
Property" sign and the section of the beck that had
been closed off with the barbed wire.

"So you're literally going to wade the rest of
the way?" Karthi asked.

"Yep," I said. "You go back. If I get caught, you
shouldn't be anywhere nearby."

"OK," she said. But for the first time I thought
something in her face suggested she might actually
like to complete the mission. "I'll take Rude Word
home then. Good luck and be careful."

Then Karthi put her hand out and I shook it.
I kneeled down and tried to take Rude Word's paw,
thinking it might be funny – like he was wishing

me luck as well. But Rude Word was a dog without tricks, even this most basic one, and he just sniffed my hand and did another of his wees.

Then Karthi slipped Rude Word's lead on and walked away without looking back.

She was one cool cucumber.

Twenty-Five

Phase 3

I scrambled down the steep bank, partly on my arse to slow my slide. All the time I was careful not to spill my cargo. The beck here was deeper, and the current was stronger. The water reached most of the way up the wellies, and the odd splash came over the top, sending a trickle down my leg. But, weirdly, the current helped me. It was pushing me on. It was like a voice telling me not to turn back, to press ahead.

The bed of the beck was in some parts slimy mud that sucked at the wellies and in other parts crunchy gravel. The gravel was much easier to walk on, so I tried to stick to that, but sometimes I'd plunge into the soft mud, and more water would flow into the wellies.

Gnats and flies buzzed and flitted over the water. I wondered if leeches lurked below. On each side, the trees and bushes were so dense I couldn't see what was going on behind them.

And then I realised I didn't know exactly where I was supposed to deposit my payload. It had to be in a place where the ecological survey people were going to look. So right where they were going to build the car park and the warehouse.

I kept peering through the trees to try to spot signs of evil industrial life. I caught the odd glimpse of houses in the distance. Sometimes I'd hear cars roar past, indicating a road.

And then I saw something very different. A willow tree had fallen half across the beck, which was annoying, as I'd have to push round it to go on. But it also created a gap I could see through. Ahead I saw a vast yellow building with XLS CONSTRUCTION written on the side of it. I didn't know much about buildings, but this hideous yellow block was clearly constructed by people who didn't care about making things look nice or blending in with nature. If for some reason you had to

design a building for people who wanted to stomp on crayfish and pee in the beck and murder slow worms, then I imagined this would be what you'd come up with.

It also gave me a target. The building was about fifty metres further along the beck. I was going to deliver the payload right there in front of it. A precision strike.

I felt my excitement and urgency grow as I approached. I was going to plant the evidence, escape, get to the hospital, tell Grandad, *save* Grandad, be a hero, everything. I could feel myself becoming taller, stronger and braver as I waded along.

And then I heard something that pulled me out of my daydreams of power and glory.

A bark.

The hard bark of a dog trained to kill and attack. OK, that was a bit harsh. A dog trained to guard. A guard dog in other words.

Where there was a guard dog, there must be guards. I crouched down and peered hard through the leaves, but I couldn't see anything. The barking

stopped, and I went on. Guard dog or not, I was too close to the end now to go back.

The beck changed again. It became calm, the current gentle. My wellies had gradually filled with water, and this seemed the right time to empty them out. There was a block of concrete on one bank, half in and half out of the water. A good place to sit. I perched on it, carefully put down my ice-cream tub and emptied both wellies.

I closed my eyes for a second, trying to relax while tuning in to the sounds of the world around me. There was the burbling of the beck – a sound I'd come to love. The breeze in the leaves above the beck. And then I focused on the birdsong. Some random chirping that I thought was just sparrows, then a pretty boring two-note *tweet-tweet*. Other scraps of birdsong came to me, but all jumbled up. I needed Grandad to explain it all, to make it clear. But he wasn't here, and it was time to move.

Twenty-Six

Catastrophe, Triumph, Disaster

I felt beside me for the ice-cream tub. But there was nothing on the concrete block.

I stood up and looked around.

Panic.

I must have knocked the tub off when I was emptying my wellies.

Calm down, I told myself. *Breathe. Focus.*

The beck would have carried the tub downstream. At least that was the right direction. I could catch the tub if I rushed. I splashed forward, not even thinking about hiding any more. The beck twisted to the right, then bent to the left.

As I rounded a bend, I heard a new sound. The gentle gurgling of the beck became something louder.

Then I saw it. The slow brown beck had become a frothing white stream.

Rapids!

Rocks stood up like broken teeth from the foaming white water.

How could I ever find my crayfish in this?

I scanned ahead, my panic turning to despair. But there it was, the ice-cream tub of hope, caught in a whirlpool. I plunged after it. Sometimes stepping on a rock, sometimes crashing down into the water, which was deeper now, stronger.

I was almost there, almost within reach, when the tub began to spin away from the whirlpool. It rose and fell down a little waterfall.

But I was gaining on it. Again, I nearly had it ... No!

By now I was raging at the beck, raging at the world. All the bad things that had happened: the crapness at school, the unhappiness at home, Grandad's illness ... I would not be beaten by them!

Again the tub was caught, again it began to spin away. I was exhausted now. I couldn't keep up the chase much longer. One last frantic effort.

I dived!

My face went right into the beck. I tasted the water the way a stickleback or bullhead or crayfish would, taking in a big mouthful of it. I was blinded, my eyes full of the murky water, but my hands landed on the prize.

I pulled myself to my feet, checking that the exoskeletons were still safely inside. Now I was literally soaked from head to foot. And bruised and battered. But determined!

And I guessed that I was pretty much exactly where I needed to be. Not only was I at the epicentre of the development, I was in the perfect environment for crayfish: white water!

I scanned the beck and saw a still pool – a place of calmness in the torrent. I went over to it and kneeled down. I opened the lid of the tub and took out a handful, carefully.

And then behind me I heard a voice.

"Well, well, what have we here?"

I turned and stared into the face of ...

Twenty-Seven

The Bogey Man

Dried Bogey!

Standing on the bank, his drooling dog by his side.

Despair flooded me again.

I looked into the guard's scraggy face. I hadn't noticed last time that he had one of those horrible little beards, just on his chin and nowhere else. He also had an earring, which I wasn't expecting.

As I stared at Dried Bogey, he stared at my ice-cream tub. I suddenly felt a bit embarrassed about it and wished Grandad had used something else. Something technical or scientific. A container made out of aluminium or laboratory-grade glass.

Dried Bogey's pale, cruel eyes took all this in.

I thought about running for it, but I'd never have escaped. I was crouched down in the water, and Dried Bogey only had to reach out to grab me. Plus, my wellies were full of water again, and you have no chance of escaping when your wellies are full of water.

There wasn't even any point in dumping the crayfish now. Bogey Face would just explain that it was a con. It had been for nothing: all of Grandad's planning, my great trek through the savage waters of the beck. The development would go ahead. The crayfish and voles were doomed, and Grandad ... Tears stung my eyes.

Dried Bogey leaned over and took the ice-cream tub from my hands quite gently. He held it up closer to his face and stared some more. And then he laughed. It wasn't really an evil laugh, just a normal one. He'd won, after all, so no wonder he was happy.

"I get it," Dried Bogey said, when his laughter came to a halt. "Don't suppose this was your idea, was it?"

I couldn't speak. I hung my head.

"Where's the old geezer?"

If I'd said "In the hospital", I'd have cried. But I had to say something. I got out a teenagery "Dunno".

And then Dried Bogey did the weirdest thing. He turned the ice-cream tub upside down, letting the shells scatter out like confetti.

"W-What are you doing?" I asked.

Dried Bogey looked at me. Then he pulled up the sleeve of his jacket and turned his wrist towards me. There was an elaborate tattoo there, swirly letters spelling out a word: SPAM.

"Spam?" I said.

"Society for the Prevention of Animal Maltreatment," he explained.

"Hang on ... What are you saying? Are you ...?"

"OK, look, quick version. SPAM was an organisation dedicated to de-oppressing our animal brothers and sisters. A big deal back in the day. But we had, er, internal divisions. The vegans weren't keen on the name SPAM, which they might have made clearer before I got the tattoo done, but there you go. Some of the group left to join the ALF ..."

"The what?" I said.

"Animal Liberation Front. Others went more mainstream – joined the RSPCA, that kind of thing. Sellouts. Louise – Lou-Lou, I called her – was the main reason I joined in the first place, and she became a yoga teacher."

"And are you still one of those?" I asked, beginning to understand what he was saying. "I mean, like, animal terrorists? Did you become a security guard just to sabotage the operation?"

"What? Nah," Dried Bogey said. "Just a job, innit? But I still have my principles. Anyway, old Bumface is a right so-and-so."

"Bumface? The other security guard? That's what we call him too!"

"Well, what else would you call him? I'm meant to get an hour for me lunch, and regular bathroom breaks, but he stands outside the gents with his stopwatch. That tells you all you need to know about Bumface. Right, you better hop it before he starts wondering where me and Tracy have got to and comes looking."

"Tracy?" I asked.

Dried Bogey smiled down at the hellhound.

"She wouldn't hurt a fly," he laughed. "Anyway, it's a good plan. Impressed." He pointed at the crayfish shells. "The survey will find these, then it'll be goodbye car park. Sweet. Now, like I said, skip it!"

"Thanks," I said. "I didn't think you'd be … I mean I thought you'd be …"

"Yeah, well, you never know what a feller's like till you talk to him. Or her."

I started wading back the way I'd come, but Dried Bogey called out, "You called Bumface 'Bumface'. So … what did you call me then?"

My mind raced, trying to find something good as a reward for Dried Bogey saving the day. What would a retired eco-warrior want to be called? I thought of some possible superheroes. Wolverine? Spider-Man?

"Legolas!" I shouted. "The cool elf from *The Lord of the Rings*."

I didn't look back, but I'd swear I could hear his crusty old face crackle as he smiled.

Twenty-Eight
The Darkest Hour

Two hours later, I was at the hospital.

I'd had to wade all the way back along the beck, then stomp in the wellies up to Grandad's. Karthi was waiting for me, her head peering over the hedge.

"And?" she asked.

"You won't believe this," I said, and then I tried to explain everything that had happened. I hardly believed it myself. Well, some bits I exaggerated, just to make the story a bit more exciting.

"Yeah, yeah," Karthi said, in that way that means "no, no". "But did you actually leave the crayfish bits at the site?"

"Exoskeletons," I corrected her.

"Whatever."

"I did."

Her look made me very happy. Karthi wasn't a person to say nice things out loud, but the little smile she gave me was like a whole Shakespeare speech: full of meaning, but a bit easier to understand.

Karthi said her mum would give me a lift to the hospital if I wanted. But I said I'd rather get the bus as I didn't want to have to explain about what I'd been doing.

I spotted Mum in the hospital waiting area. She looked tired and grey. I remembered again that she had her own medical thing going on. I hadn't thought about it because of all the trouble with Grandad. But now I did.

"Are you OK, Mum?" I said when she'd finished hugging me.

"Fine, fine," Mum said, which was a bit like Karthi's "Yeah, yeah". "Your dad's up on the ward with Grandad."

"How is he?" I asked.

"Grandad? He's ... Look, Kyle, he's poorly. Very poorly. A stroke is when one of the blood

vessels in your brain bleeds. He's ... no one knows exactly ... they have to wait and see."

"Can I go up?" I said.

"Yeah, you go. But he's not properly awake. He's ..."

"In a coma?"

"Not a coma," Mum replied. "Not really a coma. Just a ... small coma."

There were four beds in the ward. Each bed contained an old man surrounded by complicated machinery, with flashing lights and tubes going in and tubes going out. I saw Dad, and that was how I knew which of the old men was Grandad.

Dad was sitting next to Grandad, holding his hand. Grandad had an oxygen mask over his face. His eyes were closed.

Dad saw me and stood up. I walked over to them.

"Hey, Kyle," Dad said.

"How's Grandad?"

"He's, er, stable."

"Stable's good, isn't it?" I asked.

Dad nodded. "Hey, look, while you're here, I might pop down and see how your mum is."

I thought about how grey she looked.

"Yeah, great," I said. "I'll sit there. Where you were. Do what you were doing."

I meant holding Grandad's hand.

Dad left, and I sat. Grandad's hand was just lying on top of the covers, knotted and rough. His lumpy blue veins were like great worms, and his knuckles as big as snails. Grandad's hands were like some ancient sea creature. Maybe even a bit like a giant pale version of a crayfish.

I put my hand on his and then slipped my fingers underneath so that I was holding it as my dad had done.

It was cold.

Not the cold of death. But deathly cold.

"Grandad," I said, "I did it. I mean *we* did it. I took the ice-cream tub of shells – I mean exoskeletons. I walked down to the barbed wire with Karthi and Rude Word, and then I went on by myself so it doesn't ruin Karthi's legal career, and I got to the right place. Then, guess what, Dried

Bogey was there, but it turns out he's a goodie, sort of, and I planted the evidence, so it's all going to be OK."

The visitors in the ward were staring at me. Probably because I said all this while also sobbing and crying, which was pretty embarrassing.

And then I put my face on Grandad's hand, my wet tears soaking into his dry skin.

I calmed down after a few minutes and looked up at his face, hoping that I'd see his eyes open and a smile begin to form on his lips. Except he had the oxygen mask on, so I wouldn't even have been able to see it.

Then Dad came back, and it was time to go home.

Twenty-Nine

Back to the Hospital

Things were complicated the next day. My mum had another appointment at the hospital, on top of Grandad being there. So there was a lot of stuff in my head, none of which I wanted to be there.

I didn't want to go to school, but Dad said I had to. He told me to get the bus to the hospital after school, and we could all meet there. Dad made it sound like it was important, and I suppose I knew what that meant. It was Grandad. And it wasn't good news.

I tried not to think about it at school, but it must have been pretty obvious that I wasn't in the happiest of moods.

At break, I sat outside on a bench, and as I was staring into space, I felt someone come up beside me.

And of course it was Dredge. But just Dredge. No mates. As I turned to look at him, he looked at me. Dredge appeared very unDredgion. It looked like all his cockiness had been drained out of him.

"All right?" he said.

"All right," I replied.

Dredge hesitated, then spoke quickly.

"Been thinking about the other day. You and that girl. And the things you had in that box. And after. The stuff that, er, happened. And I sort of realised I'd been a ... a dick. So, er, anyway ..."

Then he trailed off.

Dredge looked strangely alone. Lonely, in fact. He was a prince stripped of his courtiers. Bullet and Whetstone must have gone off to find another jerk to follow around. I felt a bit sorry for him.

I wasn't sure why I said it, but what came out of my mouth next was, "Do you want to hang out?"

Dredge looked startled, then he said, "No, not really." And he wandered off.

*

Somehow I stumbled my way to the end of school. I got the bus straight into Leeds and walked to the hospital, feeling empty.

I was hoping to see Mum or Dad in the lobby, but it was just busy with the usual hospital people, so I took the lift up to the fourth floor. I wanted the lift to keep on going for ever, because as long as I was in it, Grandad was still OK.

The doors opened. I turned right and followed the corridor that led to the ward.

I lifted my head up, and there, just outside the ward, I saw Mum and Dad. They were hugging. Mum had her head on Dad's shoulder, her eyes closed. Then she opened them, and I saw that she'd been crying again. Mum gazed ahead without really looking. And then she saw me and pulled away from Dad and wiped her eyes with the heel of her hand.

Dad turned and saw me, and his face was something I know I'll never forget. My dad's not really an emotional person. When it comes to emotions, he's always just a bit of it – I mean a bit happy, a bit sad, a bit annoyed. But now Dad's face

was transformed. He wasn't a bit anything. He was a lot. Whatever emotion it was looked like it'd been hammered into his face, leaving it bruised and sunken.

I ran to them, and they both hugged me.

Then Mum did a kind of combined cry and laugh, and she said to me, "Kyle, we've got some news."

Her voice was ... funny. It didn't seem quite the right voice for telling me that Grandad was dead. But feeling things can do that – change what should be easy into something nearly impossible.

Then I looked at my dad again, and the big thing that he'd been feeling, the thing battered into his face, changed slightly. And it was him who told me.

"How do you like the idea of having a little brother?"

"Or sister," said Mum.

"What?" I said.

I couldn't compute. I didn't get it.

"You know me and your mum have been coming here for a few months? We should have talked to you about it, but most of the time it

doesn't work out, and we didn't want to get your hopes up. Or our hopes up."

"What are you on about?" I asked.

"Your mum's been having IVF ... you know, to make a test-tube baby. And it's worked. At last. We just found out today."

And then Dad went back to hugging Mum. It included some kissing, which was completely out of place in a hospital, or anywhere else for that matter.

"But Grandad ...?" I said, not understanding anything. I understood about the IVF of course, but I didn't really know what to do or say about it.

My mum smiled a sad smile and said, "It's OK for you to go and see him now. He's ... at peace."

Dad looked at her, his face showing something like irritation. *You shouldn't have told him*, it seemed to say.

I pushed into the ward feeling numb. The old men were still there, buried in their bleeping machines.

They hadn't moved Grandad from his bed. Just propped him up a bit. I was terrified that his eyes

might be wide open and staring, but of course they would never have left him like that.

Grandad's hands were folded on the bed in front of him.

It was time to say goodbye.

Then, just as I was about to take his cold dead hand again, Grandad's eyes popped open, and he surveyed me with his old yellow stare.

"Did you not bring me owt?" he said, his voice only a bit less loud than usual. "I believe grapes are traditional. You can keep your flowers. What use are flowers, except for looking at? I gather there's some you can eat, but that's for them in London. Anyway, lad, I'm bored stiff 'ere, so tell us your news."

Thirty

The End

When I'd got over my shock and delight that
Grandad wasn't even a bit dead, I told him
all about the adventure. He didn't remember
anything I'd said the day before.

"Nicely done, lad," was all Grandad said
about it. "Nicely done."

My mum and dad told me bits and pieces
about the IVF. Somewhere deep down I must have
known (a) that they wanted to have another kid
and (b) they were doing something about it. But
there's stuff you want to know, and stuff you don't,
and I didn't. But, yeah, I was kind of tingly-happy
about it.

Grandad was in hospital for another week.
Then he came to live with us. So did Rude Word.

Karthi and her mum were sick to death of him. Now it was our turn to be sick to death of him.

Dad said Grandad would be able to help with the childcare, which made it sound like he was going to be here for ever. Grandad said he'd only be staying a while and then he'd be back to his own house and his own shed. We'll see.

Karthi isn't my girlfriend. I'm not saying she's never going to be, and I'm definitely not saying I wouldn't quite like it if she was. But she isn't.

So Grandad came to stay with us, and him and me and Mum and Rude Word were watching the evening news. First it was the news from all over the UK and the world. Grandad wasn't ever very interested in that, unless for some reason Leeds was in it. Then it was the local news.

I could tell Grandad was tense and excited because he kept clacking his false teeth together. He must have known what was coming. But there were so many other local news stories that it didn't look like the thing that Grandad was waiting for

was going to be on. With each story about people dumping litter, or some bloke who could play the trombone while standing on their head, Grandad got more annoyed. And then the newsreader said: "And finally, we report on the plan to create warehousing and parking along the Wykebeck in Leeds ..."

I turned back to Grandad again. The beck! As the newsreader continued, Grandad's face flooded with emotion. He beamed at me and nodded, and his eyes said it all. *We did it!*

Our books are tested
for children and young people by
children and young people.

Thanks to everyone who consulted on
a manuscript for their time and effort in
helping us to make our books better
for our readers.

Discover Anthony McGowan's award-winning quartet about brothers Nicky and Kenny.

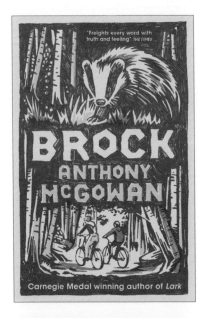

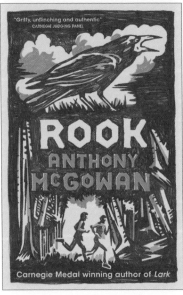

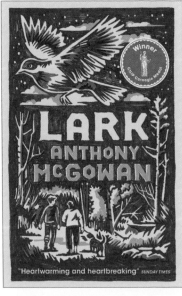